MW00805198

A Lye Soap Bath

Little Stinker Series
Book 3

Dave Sargent was born and raised on a dairy farm in
northwest Arkansas. When he began writing in 1990, he
made a decision to dedicate the remainder of his life to
encouraging children to read and write. He is very good
with students and teachers alike. He and his wife Pat
travel across the United States together. They write
about animals with character traits. They are good at
showing how animals act a lot like kids.

A Lye Soap Bath

Little Stinker Series
Book 3

By Dave Sargent

Illustrated by Elaine Woodward

Ozark Publishing, Inc.
P.O. Box 228
Prairie Grove, AR 72753

Cataloging-in-Publication Data

Sargent, Dave, 1941–
    A lye soap bath / by Dave Sargent ;
illustrated by Elaine Woodward. —Prairie
Grove, AR : Ozark Publishing, c2007.
    p. cm. (Little stinker series ; 3)

    "Be truthful"—Cover.
    SUMMARY: When Dave's mom finds
the baby skunks he had hidden under his bed,
she grabs the belt and folds it in half. Hard
licks follow.
    ISBN 1-59381-279-5 (hc)
            1-59381-280-9 (pbk)

    1. Skunks—Juvenile fiction.
2. Dogs—Juvenile fiction.
[1. Games—Fiction.]
I. Woodward, Elaine, 1956– ill.
II. Title. III. Series.

    PZ7.S243Ly 2007
    [Fic]—dc21   2005906109

Copyright © 2007 by Dave Sargent
All rights reserved

Printed in the United States of America

iv

Inspired by

the baby skunks I found when I was seven years old. I took them home with me and hid them in my room.

Dedicated to

any parent who has had his/her mouth washed out with lye soap!

Foreword

When Dave's mom finds the baby skunks he has hidden under his bed, she grabs the belt and folds it in half. Hard licks follow.

Contents

If you'd like to have Dave Sargent, the author of the Little Stinker Series, visit your school free of charge, call: 1-800-321-5671.

One

Lye Soap and Tomato Juice

When Mom sent me outside with my plate, I sat down on the front porch and ate the rest of my supper. When I had finished eating, I started back in the house.

Mom met me at the door and took my plate. She handed me a bar of lye soap and a jar of tomato juice. She told me to scrub up with the lye soap first. Then I was to rub the tomato juice all over me. And then, I was to wash off the tomato juice before I came back in the house.

By the time I got cleaned up and back in the house, it was bedtime. My brothers were heading up the stairs and I fell right in behind them. All three of us had to sleep in the same bed. We no sooner got in bed when Emery and Jack started yelling, "Mama! It stinks up here!"

Momma yelled back, "You boys quiet down and go to sleep."

Just like all kids, we didn't like going to bed. A few minutes later, Emery jumped out of bed and sailed down the stairs.

He said, "Mama, it smells so bad up there that I can't stand it! I'd rather sleep outside with the dog!"

Mama met him at the foot of the stairs.

She said, "Come back upstairs with me, Emery. I'll find out what you're talking about."

Two

The Search

Mama and Emery came up the stairs. Mama no sooner than got to the top of the stairs when she said, "Phewee! I smell it, too! Dave, have you had a skunk up here?"

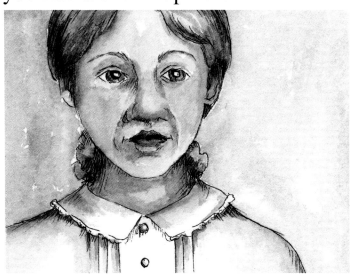

"No, Mama," I replied.

"Take your clothes and hang them on the clothesline! And don't you ever mess with a skunk again!" Mama warned.

"Okay, Mama," I replied. I put on some clean clothes and, using the broom handle, pushed all my dirty clothes inside a paper sack. I took the sack outside and pinned my clothes on the clothesline. I went back inside, up the stairs and slipped into bed. It wasn't two minutes until both Emery and Jack jumped out of bed. They ran down the stairs screaming, "Mama, it smells worse up there!"

Again, Mama came upstairs. When she reached the top of the stairs, she shook her head.

"Where's the skunk, Dave?" she demanded. "There's no way it can smell this bad up here because of clothes. I want to know where the skunk is, and I want to know now!"

"I don't know anything about a skunk, Mama," I replied.

Mama said, "You're lying to me, Dave. And you know what happens when you lie."

"I know what happens, Mama, but I'm not lying," I said.

"Have it your way. But the truth will come out. And when it does, you'll be in trouble," she said loudly.

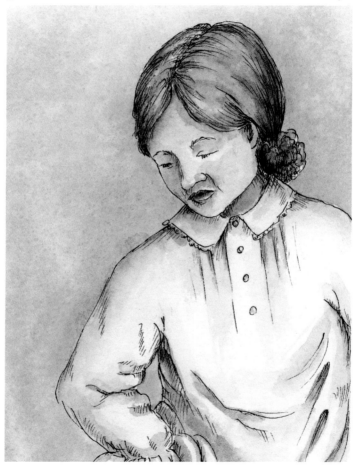

Three

Eight Hard Licks

Mama began searching the room. She looked through our boxes. She searched through all the dresser drawers. She searched the room and never found a thing.

I smiled, thinking she'd never find them. I could tell Mama was stumped. She stood in the middle of the room, shook her head and looked around. She was thinking real hard. Then she muttered, "I don't get it. I've looked everywhere."

She started toward the stairs. Then she turned and looked at the bed. "Aha! Under the bed!" she said. "I didn't look under the bed!"

She knelt down on the floor so that she could see under the bed. Well, what can I say? I was in a whole lot of trouble.

Mama pulled the shoe box out from under the bed. When she took the lid off of the box, she muttered, "Oh my Lord!" She was trying hard to look and act real mad, through a half-smile and a half-laugh.

The first thing she did was grab a belt. She folded it in half and gave me six very hard licks.

"Those licks were for lying!" she said. Then she gave me two more licks. "Those licks were for bringing the skunks into the house."

Then she threw the belt on the dresser, shook her finger at me and said, "Get those skunks out of this house! Take them back where you got them and don't come back until you do!"

I lowered my head and said "Okay, Mama."

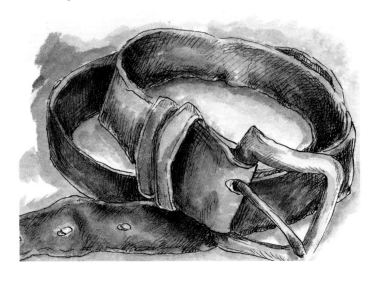

Four

Skunk Facts

A skunk has musk glands and can shoot a liquid that smells a lot like rotten eggs. It usually gives a warning before it sprays. It stamps the ground with its front feet, snaps its teeth and its hairs stand up. Then it swings its rear end around, lifts its tail and shoots!

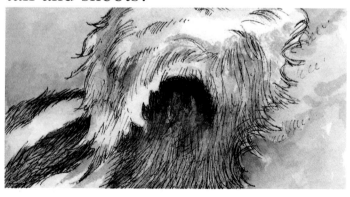